LAUGHS AND TEARS GALORE!

Stories and poems with twists by Heather and Tony Flood

LAUGHS AND TEARS GALORE!

Stories and poems with twists

Published in the UK in March, 2022 by Tony Flood in conjunction with SW Communications.

ISBN: 9798428865561

CREDITS

COVERS DESIGNED by:
Emmy Ellis https://studioenp.com/

CREATOR OF IMAGE ON FRONT COVER:
len_pri@depositphotos

CONTENTS FORMATTED by:
James Harvey - Badgoose Publishing
soulsong.co.uk

PRAISE FOR

LAUGHS AND TEARS GALORE!

DELIGHTFUL! Heather and Tony Flood have come up with a delightful and intriguing collection of poems and short stories to keep you reading through the night. The poetry is diverse and thought-provoking, and the short stories have twists in the tale to keep you guessing. **- Ellie Dean, author of international best-selling Cliffehaven series.**

INTRIGUING! Tony and Heather have opened their Floodgates so that you are awash with a wide mixture of poems and short stories to intrigue on tides of surprises. These talented authors have launched a ship on a sea of words to perhaps make your eyes water with waves of smiles and tears. They'll take you swimmingly along through the currents without drowning your thoughts and expectations. **- Laurie Wilkinson, author of ten popular poetry books embracing everyday life and feelings, with donations from sales going to Help for Heroes.**

ENTHRALLING! A fascinating variety of well-constructed short stories and poems, with depth and variety, which keep you guessing. It's great to be surprised and I certainly was. This light-hearted look at human foibles is endearing and very entertaining. **- Jim Whelan, actor and author.**

CAPTIVATING! WOW! What a delight! My only disappointment was reaching the end... I wanted more! There's not always time to concentrate on a novel - so these 'bite-sized' captivating stories and poems were an ideal accompaniment to a cup of tea when taking a break on a busy day. **- Daisy Bourne, author of Tales of Avalon series.**

YOU QUALIFY FOR A FREE BOOK

As a 'thank you' for buying Laughs and Tears Galore!, authors Heather and Tony Flood are offering you one of their other books FREE.

To obtain a complimentary e-version just choose one of the books from the lists on pages 128 and 130. Then email your choice to Tony at tflood04@yahoo.co.uk and he will email you back with the e-version as an attachment.

The authors make donations to Children with Cancer UK from paperback sales. You can help by writing a review if you enjoy them.

ACKNOWLEDGEMENTS

Heather and Tony would like to thank authors Ellie Dean, Laurie Wilkinson, Jim Whelan and Daisy Bourne for their excellent endorsements - and Tamara McKinley, Rose Twidell and John Newton for their very helpful feedback.

Many thanks also to James Harvey of Badgoose Publishing and Emmy Ellis of Studioenp for their first class formatting and cover designs respectively.

CONTENTS

IF YOU LET IT,
a poem by Heather Flood

There's always something to wreck your day,

some obstruction to mar your way,

a thought to change blue skies to grey –

If you let it.

There's always something to spoil your fun,

disturb your mind when the day is done.

A cloud that threatens to hide the sun –

If you let it.

Ignore what upsets you, the stones and stings,

find something good in whatever life brings.

Life will surround you with wonderful things –

If you let it.

LEARNING FROM HENRY'S MISTAKE,
a short story by Tony Flood

Henry Goldsmith felt very pleased with himself. He had spent the early part of a cold November evening in the arms of his mistress in her ground-floor flat. Now, two hours later, he prepared to address a meeting on his specialist subject, conservation and global warming.

About 40 people had gathered in an Eastbourne church hall for the meeting and they applauded loudly when he was introduced.

Henry began: "Global warming is doing so much damage by increasing the Earth's average surface temperature due to an over-emittance of greenhouse gases that collect in the atmosphere. This traps the sun's heat and causes the planet to warm."

As Henry, a 35-year-old scientific researcher,

continued, he became aware of the door opening at the back of the hall and a late-comer entering.

He looked up, surprised to see it was his wife Amanda.

Trying to regain his concentration, Henry went on: "We can all help by saving energy. One simple way to do this is to turn off the lights when we leave a room or put them on dim if we don't need the room to be fully lit."

Henry felt alarm as he saw that Amanda, instead of quietly taking a seat, had marched boldly forward to stand in front of him.

Worse still, his normally shy wife shouted angrily: "You make me sick Henry Goldsmith. Our marriage is over."

"What's this about, darling?" he asked, bewildered. "Why are you embarrassing me like this?"

Amanda's flinty grey eyes glared at him. "Because of your womanizing. The private detective I hired to follow you has just brought me photographic proof that you were misbehaving with your mistress in her apartment earlier this evening. Not only are you an adulterer, you're a fool and a hypocrite. You and your woman friend were so eager that you got undressed with the lights on and the curtains open! Obviously you were not concerned at the time with saving energy and global warming!"

Everyone present would long remember Henry's mistake - and the value of turning off lights when not required.

JUST A BOY 0F 18 ON D-DAY,
a poem by Heather Flood

I was 18, on a boat with my mate Tommy,

sailing out to sea.

If my dear old dad Bill knew,

he would be so proud of me.

He died in the First World War,

torpedoed with his crew,

They were protecting the ships

that brought the food for you.

The day came when we also went to fight,

and said goodbye to our mums,

"See you, and don't worry,

we'll look after each other, we're chums."

It was now our turn, we had to go,

kit bags at the ready,

In stormy seas, with my weak knees,

it wasn't easy to keep steady.

We went to war, feeling quite scared,

sailing from Plymouth Quay.

Two young boys, who'd joined the Navy,

my mate Tommy and me.

We heard the guns,

we saw the planes roaring overhead,

But I didn't see the bullet that

shot poor Tommy dead.

He paid the price, bless his heart,

I could not save my friend.

We'd both been willing to fight

side by side until the very end.

No time to grieve, or shed a tear,

for Tommy, the mate I'd lost,

Just one of the boys who died that day.

What a terrible cost.

I'm an old man now, sailing back to France,

in the choppy sea.

Remembering when I went to war,

with Tommy from Plymouth Quay.

As we approach the beach today,

there are no bodies bobbing around.

The water is clean, no blood to be seen

and no one dead on the ground.

Now we sail once more to remember,

and salute you with pride and regret.

The friends we lost, in the sea they were tossed,

as if we could ever forget.

AN AMAZING ESCAPE,
a short story by Tony Flood

I t was the moment for which 18-year-old Niki Forster had been working so hard.

The talented young singer had been shortlisted by the highly respected Westmore Operatic Society for the title role in Madame Butterfly - and now it was her turn to sing at the auditions they were holding in the National Youth Theatre, North London.

But, as Niki opened her folder to place her musical score on the stand in front of the orchestra, she gasped in disbelief. The music was not there!

She heard a noise and glanced across to see her main rival for the role, Geraldine Montgomery, in the wings, appearing to stifle a chuckle. When the girl's freckled face betrayed a smirk, Niki immediately thought that Geraldine must have taken the score.

The orchestra started to play the introduction to 'One Fine Day', and Niki realised she would have to sing the piece from memory. But, in her panic, she mistimed the opening notes before calling upon her inner strength and recovering to give an exhilarating performance.

It earned applause from the director, Sir Derek Favisham, and other members of the Operatic Society, sat in the stalls, listening to the auditions.

As she left the stage Niki felt greatly relieved to have got through her ordeal so well, but realised her performance could have been better.

In contrast, Geraldine's rendition was technically perfect, and she was given the part.

Niki was shattered. She ran to one of the dressing rooms, not wanting anyone to see the tears running down her cheeks. Her grief was interrupted by a knock on the door. Niki tried to ignore it, but the voice of Sir Derek Favisham called out "Niki, I'd like to talk to you."

The distressed young woman wiped away smudged mascara with the last two tissues she carried and tried to compose her attractive features.

Sir Derek, a tall, charismatic, balding man in his late fifties, was most sympathetic when Niki explained that her musical score had suddenly gone missing.

"That's awful," he said. "Do you know how it happened?"

She was tempted to tell him about the smirking Geraldine, who'd been standing near the chair on which the music folder was left before the auditions started. But as there was no proof that Geraldine had taken the music, Niki remained silent, and simply shook her head.

After a brief pause, Sir Derek resumed speaking. "Unfortunately, the decision has been made and Geraldine is to play Madame Butterfly. The other leading roles have also been cast, but I could offer you a supporting part if you'd like to come to rehearsals tomorrow."

"That's very kind of you, Sir Derek, but I'd rather not."

"Are you sure, Niki? It will mean you missing our trip to New York to give a performance next month. It's going to be a prestigious production."

"I know, but I'm just not in the right state of mind to throw myself into rehearsals at the moment and I don't want to let you down." Niki also felt there would be friction between her and Geraldine.

Sir Derek nodded, sighed and departed.

Niki again dissolved into tears. She went in search of tissues in the now empty dressing room next door which had been used by Geraldine.

There were no tissues, but in the wastepaper basket two screwed up sheets of paper were plainly visible. It was her musical score; complete with the markings she had made in a felt-tipped pen.

11

When Niki eventually left the theatre, she could see Geraldine laughing and joking with two of her friends outside. Far from showing any sign of guilt at sabotaging her rival's audition, a cocky Geraldine called across to her: "Better luck next time, darling" The words sounded insincere and hollow.

Niki was inconsolable in the three weeks that followed. She managed to fulfil her duties as a hotel receptionist despite not being her normal bubbly self and spent most of her free time moping about at home.

"You idiot," she chided. "Even a supporting role in a New York production would have been an achievement. You've missed out on a great opportunity."

A few weeks later, while Niki sat staring into space in her lounge, a news flash came on the television. The newsreader's words jolted her.

A gunman, armed with a rifle, had been

responsible for a shooting in New York. The fatal event had occurred at the Westmore Operatic Society's performance of Madame Butterfly.

The newsreader said: "The crazed gunman yelled out 'Die you whore', presumably a reference to the fact Madame Butterfly was a geisha, and shot dead the girl who was playing the part. He continued shooting, wounding four other members of the cast."

Niki was consumed with deep feelings of horror, distress and sorrow.

When the tragic news had finally sunk in, the anguish she had felt at not landing the part of her dreams had completely vanished to be replaced by sheer relief.

The trick Geraldine had played unwittingly saved Niki's life and cost Geraldine hers.

THE BUTTERFLY AND
THE BUFFALO,
a poem by Heather Flood

The butterfly and the buffalo

met one sunny day,

she landed on his nose

as he trudged along the way.

A very unlikely pairing,

their friends at once declared,

as the butterfly balanced delicately,

not appearing to be scared.

To him she was most beautiful,

to her he was so strong,

their bond was unbreakable,

surely nothing could go wrong.

But a butterfly's life is short,

her beauty began to wane,

the buffalo knew he'd lose her

and in his heart was pain.

The day she went away

was the saddest in his life,

the butterfly and the buffalo,

a husband and a wife.

SCHOOL EXAMS,
a poem by Tony Flood

Now exams are finally done

Life once more should be such fun.

No more planning, no more plotting

No more weekends spent at swotting.

No more mornings in the chair

Almost pulling out our hair.

Wishing that we could remember

What we had learned back in November.

Yes, now exams are finally done,

Life once more should be such fun.

So why do we sit here and fret

About the marks we might not get!

HEAVEN OR HELL?
A short story by Heather Flood

I have been here in the unknown for 20 minutes, and there are quite a few of us in the line awaiting our fates.

Let me explain. I died yesterday, quietly slipped away in my bed, with no fuss and no great pain.

On that last day all my family had gathered round to say how much they loved me and would miss me.

Aimee, my granddaughter, held my hand in those last moments and whispered "Goodbye, Nan, I love you." We had built quite a bond, enjoying each other's company, laughing together. "Guess what, Nan!" she would say, and I'd listen with pride as she told me her latest achievements at school.

She got on well with everyone - except her brother Tim. They were like chalk and cheese. They made me laugh in their different ways and I loved them both dearly.

A few years later another brother arrived, little Bobby. He was so cute and, as he got older, saw himself as the peacemaker. He would try to end the arguments involving Aimee and Tim by saying "Guys, guys, let's all be friends."

If I'd had the energy, I would have willed myself to stay with Aimee and her little brothers longer, but I'd had my time. I tried to shout out "Goodbye everyone, I love you," but it was too late.

WHOOSH! I felt myself being pulled along, as if sucked into a vacuum cleaner. The sensation changed and I began to relax as I found myself floating through some sort of dark tunnel. Everything seemed peaceful until sparkling white lights appeared, popping up as I glided along. POW! - there was an explosion of bright colours and I suddenly found myself standing in a line with other people waiting.

There isn't a mirror in this new place to which I

have been sent so I can't look at myself, but I seem to be wearing my best dress, and those really nice black shoes I bought last year for a Christmas party. How strange, since I had died in bed with a pink nightdress on.

We move further along the tunnel until we come to a man in a white uniform, handing out forms and pens.

We have been given a questionnaire headed 'PREFERRED CHOICES'. It asks me to pick from 'heaven' or 'other'. I select 'heaven'.

Then I'm asked 'male or female?' I tick 'female'. I wouldn't want to change as I've always loved being a mother and grandmother. And I've greatly enjoyed talking ten to the dozen and shopping till I drop.

When it comes to 'married or single?' I put 'married'. I've had two husbands, one a 'scoundrel' and the second a lovely, caring man, with a wonderful sense of humour, who made me laugh every day until he passed away. Will I see him again? I hope so.

Next question: Choose one of the following: Mary Poppins, Ebenezer Scrooge or Lord Voldemort.

Voldemort? How did he get on this form? The only thing I like about the nasty J.K. Rowling character is that Ralph Fiennes played him in the Harry Potter film series and he's a dish.

I take a chance and put 'Lord Voldemort' in the hope I'll one day meet Ralph Fiennes.

I think this question is only a bit of fun anyway and I'd love to have a magic wand. Flying on a broomstick would also be great!

Well, that's done - form finished and handed in! Now I'm waiting in another line of people. God, I'm fed up (oh, sorry, he might be listening). Hey, wait a minute, my shoes have changed into fluffy blue slippers - I've not had a pair like this for years.

I decide to try an experiment. I turn my thoughts to my nice silver strappy sandals, which are in a box in my wardrobe at home - they now seem to be on my feet.

So, that's it. I am only imagining myself in clothes. Does that mean I'm actually naked?

I am now floating - what am I? Scotch mist?

But I'm not frightened. I have made my choices on the form and am excited about what is in store for me.

We proceed to a huge white complex. Suddenly three large holes appear in front of us. One is blue, the second yellow and the third bright red.

Another man in a white uniform appears and makes an announcement. He says that anyone who chose Mary Poppins on their form should stand in front of the blue hole and can slide straight into heaven.

Anyone who chose Ebenezer Scrooge must line-up next to the yellow hole.

The man explains: "If you selected Scrooge, you will be given other questions to answer to see if you are likely to change and deserve redemption."

Oh dear, I'm starting to feel uneasy!

The man then declares that those who put down Lord Voldemort should stand in front of the red hole. It seems I may have made the wrong choice!

What am I supposed to do now? I move forward and look down to see an even bigger hole opening up beneath me.

"What does it mean?" I ask the guy in the white uniform.

"You must jump into the hole and find out," he says. His blank expression gives nothing away.

Well, here goes! I've played it safe and tried to follow the right path all my life, but maybe everything is about to change.

At least there should be some big characters down here and, if I'm given a magic wand, I may be able to have some fun with them.

Bye, bye.

Expelliarmus!

WEEEEEEEEEEEEEEEEEEEEEEEEEEEEEEEEEE
EEEEEEEEEEEEEEEEEEEeeeeeeeee!

DEAR OLD ENGLAND,
a poem by Heather Flood

Dear Old England,

as it used to be,

when we left our doors open,

and drank cups of tea.

Dear Old England,

where the streets we walked were clean,

overloaded bins,

gum on pavements, never seen.

Dear Old England,

we loved our roast chicken lunch,

now it's Bolognese,

curry or McDonald's special brunch.

Dear Old England,

does anyone really care?

Pensioners freeze to death,

food banks everywhere.

Dear Old England,

we whisper in the dark,

not allowed to say the things we feel,

have we lost that spark?

Dear Old England,

where did our traditional values go?

We took you for granted,

when we should have loved you so.

CHRISTMAS JOY,
a poem by Heather Flood

O Christmas, lovely Christmas,

it makes us feel so jolly.

As we sing our Christmas Carols,

amongst the ornaments and holly.

The crunch, crunch, crunch,

of Wellington boots, trudging through the snow.

Glittering Christmas candles,

each one with a special glow.

Silver bells that tinkle,

little faces bright with joy.

Hearts filled with a loving feeling,

for every girl and boy.

JIMMY'S BIRTHDAY TREAT,
a short story by Tony Flood

Jimmy Musgrove sat on his favourite armchair in his cosy Eastbourne home reflecting how his nephew Paul had promised him a day to remember.

Paul, a professional photographer who seemed to have a never-ending supply of gorgeous lady friends, had asked his elderly uncle if there was anything special he wanted to do on his forthcoming 70th birthday.

"Anything?" Jimmy had said, jokingly with a sly grin, rubbing his stubbly chin.

'Yes, anything, Uncle."

"Well, since your Aunt Mary died, I have missed female company. I've missed it a lot. And I do envy you being surrounded by all those glamorous ladies. Why don't you invite a couple of them to have a threesome with me?"

He had been speaking partly in jest, but his nephew immediately agreed.

"I'll do it," Paul had promised, returning the smile with a wink. "Your birthday is next Tuesday so I'll invite Jill and Amanda over that day. They like to play around. They do acting as well as modelling and they're up for anything. You'll love them. Actually, I'm on my way to see the girls now to deliver some pictures I took of them for their portfolio and an advertisement."

Paul had the photos in an envelope with him, and when he showed Jimmy, his uncle was bowled over, especially with shots of the two sexy women in skimpy bikinis in front of a tropical backdrop.

"The collection is called 'The Other Side' Paul explained. 'They're supposed to be from the other side of the world."

"Wow!" Jimmy had said, his moustache bristling. "I'm all for sampling the other side. But do you think they'll be prepared to indulge an old guy like me?"

He realised that although he looked a lot younger than his age, they might not fancy cavorting with a 70-year-old Bruce Forsyth look-alike.

"Age means nothing to them," Paul had insisted, his handsome features creasing into a reassuring smile.

Paul phoned on Sunday to confirm the arrangement, but then dropped a bombshell. He mentioned that he'd told his father he was fulfilling Jimmy's wish to play around with two dolly birds.

"Damn!" muttered Jimmy. "Your father can't keep anything to himself - he'll tell everyone."

"Don't worry," his nephew soothed. "He thinks you are to be admired."

Jimmy saw things differently People would sit in judgement of him, and his reputation would be tarnished.

Oh, the shame of it! He considered calling the whole thing off, but the damage had been done.

When Tuesday arrived Jimmy opened his

birthday cards and read his Facebook messages, but his thoughts were mainly on the treat Jill and Amanda would be providing.

He took an hour to get ready. After soaking himself in the bath, he shaved off his stubble, trimmed his moustache, splashed deodorant all over himself, put on his best blue shirt and smarmed down his thinning hair with the last drops from an old bottle of Brylcreem.

Jimmy then sat in his armchair, reflecting that he was just half an hour away from his wildest fantasy becoming reality. He had never taken part in a threesome, and hoped he would be up to it. Just thinking about Jill and Amanda in their undies was driving him mad.

Paul had said the ladies would come at 11am, and when they had still not arrived by 11.20 the old man became agitated. He walked across to his lounge window and stood, peering through the curtains.

Finally a car drew up. And when the doorbell rang Jimmy was almost overcome with excitement.

Upon opening the front door, he was greeted by his nephew.

"Hi Uncle Jimmy," Paul said. "Unfortunately, Jill and Amanda got held up in Manchester following a corporate event."

"Does that mean they're not coming?"

"It's OK. I picked them up from the airport and they're in my car outside. I'll join you as well to make it a foursome."

"A foursome?" mumbled Jimmy.

"Yes. It will add a bit more spice. Now don't hang around. We've got to get to the club."

"The club?" Jimmy queried.

"Yes. We're due off the first tee at 12.30 so grab your golf clubs and we'll get going."

ALL WE COULD EVER WANT,
a poem by Heather Flood

A millionaire with surplus cash,

I know I'll never be,

but with my dear ones by my side,

this does not bother me.

I'm sure it's true

for many families everywhere,

we've riches galore

if we have love to share.

THE EMPTY BEACH,
a poem by Heather Flood

The beach was empty, the sea very cold

The sun was setting, turning all to gold.

Seagulls called with their eerie cry

Soaring overhead in the evening sky.

A man and his dog walked along by the tower

He looked unhappy, his face was sour.

His wife had left him, his children, too

It was just him and the dog as friends were few.

He was sorry his life had come to this

When once it seemed like all was bliss.

Simply because of one silly row

Everything would be different now.

As he sat reflecting, throwing pebbles in the sea

The dog came beside him and climbed on his knee.

The faithful spaniel licked the hand of his friend

His dog would be with him right up to the end.

NO-BRAINER,
a short story by Tony Flood

Susie Temple soon began to realise why bumptious businessman Roger Manning had invited her out. His whole demeanour made it clear to the former model that he saw her simply as a 'trophy' - and wasn't interested in what she had to say.

He talked almost non-stop, but it was AT her rather than TO her. So it gave the 30-year-old blonde great satisfaction to briefly shut him up with a tantalising glimpse of her thighs when she eased her way slowly out of his two-seater Mazda MX-5.

Roger was taking her horse racing at Fontwell Park on their second date, but first they were stopping off at the fashion house he owned in Lewes. After quickly giving his staff instructions about some new designs, he was held up by a disgruntled man complaining about a sports jacket.

"Look," said the indignant middle-aged balding man, taking the tweed jacket out of the bag he was carrying. "I've discovered a small hole in it. That's not normal wear and tear. I want a replacement or my money back."

"Have you got the receipt, sir?" asked Roger.

"No, I haven't kept it."

"Did you purchase it by credit or debit card?" Roger queried.

"No, I paid cash," said the man.

"Then you have no proof of purchase," replied Roger with the trace of a smile. "And we cannot exchange something without proof of purchase. Now if you'll excuse me." He turned away from the man, and swept Susie out to his bright red sports car.

"You've lost a customer there," she said as they drove off.

"Too bad!" Roger retorted. "He should have kept the receipt. It's a no-brainer."

They quickly left the town behind, and Susie became captivated by the picturesque countryside as they sped along to make up for lost time.

"I just love Sussex - it's beautiful," Susie enthused. But as she spoke, they encountered a traffic jam and her impatient companion snapped: "Never mind about beautiful Sussex - let's find an alternative route."

He gave her a map, but she missed the turn off, which caused him to rant: "I can't believe you didn't spot that turn - it was a no-brainer."

They arrived late and rushed from the car park into the course to find they had missed the first race.

Susie expected Roger to take them to the restaurant for lunch, or at least order her a drink from the bar. He did neither! Instead, he led the way to the parade ring to run his eye over the horses in the next race.

Beads of sweat started to form on his rotund face

as he pushed through the crowd. "See that horse, there," he bellowed, pointing a podgy finger at it. "That's going to win - I've been given a tip from a trainer, and it looks in great shape. Let's go and get a bet on."

But they'd moved only a few steps when a tall, imposing man bowled up to them. "Roger," he boomed. "I'm so pleased to bump into you. I'm handling a big deal that I know you're going to be interested in."

"Hello, Oswald," Roger said, in an agitated tone.

"Aren't you going to introduce me to this lovely lady?" asked Oswald.

"Her name's Susie," Roger answered coolly. "Susie, this is my business associate Oswald Gardner. Look, just give me a minute, Oswald." Roger turned to Susie and thrust a bundle of notes into her hand. "I want you to put a bet on for me," he said.

"What do I have to do?" she asked, doubtfully.

"Just go to the Tote betting booths over there," he rasped, gesturing towards them. "Bet £100 to win on Burlesque. Got that? £100 to win on Burlesque. Make sure you get a betting slip."

Susie still appeared uncertain.

"Look, it's a no-brainer," he assured her, repeating his favourite phrase. "Now hurry up and get the best odds you can."

With that, he gave her a push in the right direction and began talking to Oswald.

Susie joined the queue at one of the betting booths. A young man immediately in front of her started chatting and by the time she got to the front Susie had forgotten the name of the horse Roger asked her to back.

"What bet do you want to make, lady?" inquired the bookie. She was struck dumb. "Come on, love, we haven't got all day," he urged.

What was it Roger had said? 'Bet £100 to win' But what was the name of the damn horse? The only other thing she could remember was that he had told her to get the best odds. So she asked: "What horse are you giving the best odds on?"

"That would be Beautiful Sussex," said the man, impatiently. "It's 100-1, love."

That name rang a bell - she remembered Roger saying it. "OK. I want to put £100 to win on Beautiful Sussex."

Susie hurried back to find Roger deep in conversation with Oswald. "Did you put the bet on?" he asked.

"Yes," she said. "And I got you great odds."

"Good," he replied, giving her a slight smile.

"Yes," Susie beamed at him. "I got 100-1 on Beautiful Sussex."

"WHAT!" he exploded. "You stupid fool! You were supposed to put the bet on the favourite Burlesque. It was a no-brainer!"

"I'm sorry, Roger," she said, fretfully. "I remembered it began with a 'B' and we'd talked about beautiful Sussex in the car, so I got muddled."

Oswald started to giggle. "It's a simple mistake," he said sarcastically and burst out laughing.

That infuriated Roger even more. When Susie offered him the betting slip, he snapped: "That's no use to me - the nag you've backed stands as much chance as you do of winning Mastermind. Just clear off out of my sight, you idiot."

She looked at him in shock.

"Go - I don't ever want to see you again," he shouted.

Susie saw red - and so did Roger because she delivered a stinging slap across his face. "You rude, pompous ass!" she retorted before departing with the betting slip still in her other hand.

Her first instinct was to leave the course straight away, but she decided to watch the race first. She squeezed past several punters until she was almost standing on the rails of the track, just a minute before the start.

"Which one is Beautiful Sussex?" Susie asked the man next to her.

"The grey horse that won't get into the stalls," he said. "If you've backed that you've thrown your money away."

"Oh," she muttered, disappointed and embarrassed. "And what have you backed?"

"I've put £100 to win on Burlesque. I got odds of 2-1 on the Tote," he said proudly.

"That's exactly the bet my boyfriend wanted me to do," Susie told him. "But I got odds of 100-1 on Beautiful Sussex instead. He wasn't very pleased."

"No wonder," remarked the man with a smile.

At that moment the race started. It seemed her new companion was right because Beautiful Sussex was in last place and for the first mile made no progress while Burlesque set the pace.

But in the second mile the grey horse began to move up, swiftly overtaking three of the other backmarkers.

As Susie watched in astonishment, two of the leading horses collided when landing badly over a hurdle and, with three furlongs to go, Beautiful Sussex was in second place.

Burlesque still seemed to have the race won but stumbled on a divot as the finishing line beckoned, and Beautiful Sussex sensationally snatched first place by a short head.

"I don't believe it!" exclaimed the man next to her. He stormed off and threw his betting slip away in disgust. The wind blew it in Susie's face.

She could not believe the rank outsider she'd backed had actually won until it was announced on the Tannoy. And at 100-1, the bet she had placed was worth £10,000.

'What should I do?' Susie thought. 'Look for Roger and give him the betting slip? Or cash it in myself and make a quick exit?' It seemed to be a no-brainer!

After collecting the winnings in £50 notes, Susie

was about to telephone for a taxi when she saw Roger and Oswald approaching. "Oh, no," she muttered as they forced their way through the crowd after spotting her. She was tempted to hurry away, but decided to face them.

"I believe you have something belonging to me," Roger said.

"Do I?" she asked, feigning innocence. "And what would that be?"

"Either my winnings or the betting slip if you haven't cashed it in," he replied in a blunt, business-like tone.

"But you said you didn't want the betting slip when I tried to give it to you," Susie pointed out.

"That was because you backed the wrong damn horse," he snapped.

"Don't you mean the right horse?" Oswald chided.

"This is no time for joking, Oswald," Roger said, glaring at his friend. "This stupid blonde bimbo is trying to rob me of £10,000. Look, I can see the money sticking out of the bag she's carrying."

"Calling me a stupid blonde bimbo is going to cost you big time," Susie told him, her blue eyes blazing. "I was considering sending you what's in my bag, but not now you've insulted me."

"I want what belongs to me," Roger demanded.

"And you shall have it," she replied.

Susie fished in her pocket and pulled out a betting slip. "Here," she said, handing it to Oswald. "Please give this to Roger - I can't bear to even touch him."

"What the devil is it?" Roger wanted to know.

"It's a betting slip recording £100 placed to win on Burlesque," Oswald informed him.

"Now we are all square," said Susie.

"What you've given me is worthless," stormed Roger. "This is a con trick. Somehow you've switched betting slips. Don't think I'm falling for it. I'll sue you - this is a criminal offence."

"No it isn't," Susie protested.

"Tell her, Oswald," Roger urged. "You're a solicitor - tell her how she'll be done for fraud."

"I don't think she will, actually," his friend said calmly.

"You must be joking!" the baffled businessman exploded.

"Calm down, Roger, or you'll give yourself a heart attack. I was there when you asked Susie to put £100 to win on Burlesque and she has now given you a Tote slip for that bet. I don't think there's a court in the country that would uphold your claim."

"There!" said Susie triumphantly.

"But you've tricked me," shouted Roger.

"How could you possibly believe that I'd be capable of doing that?" she asked. "Only a few seconds ago you said I was a stupid blonde bimbo. When Oswald hands you that betting slip I think I've fulfilled what you asked me to do. You wanted proof of a wager of £100 on Burlesque and you've got it."

Oswald handed his stunned companion the

betting slip. "There you are, mate," he chuckled. "It seems you greatly underestimated this delightful young lady. She's outsmarted you."

"But she's got my money," spluttered Roger, pointing to the bulging bag in Susie's hand.

"This is mine," she said, taking out a handful of notes from her little pink bag and fanning them out. "Look at all the money I've won."

Susie may have forgotten the name of the horse, but she'd remembered what Roger had said earlier about how important it was to keep proof of purchase. So she'd picked up the betting slip the punter had thrown away, and given it to Roger. It really was another no-brainer!

COVID CURSE AND
THE TIME WE'VE LOST,
a poem by Heather Flood

Covid's a killer, it travels around,

upon the breeze, it makes no sound.

We've been locked in our homes, with fear and doubt.

We had to stay inside; we couldn't go out.

Being in lockdown was becoming a bore,

we didn't want to go out and break the law.

Who'd have thought shopping would be fun,

just popping out to buy a cream bun.

Someone to chat with would be nice,

but 'Alexa', bless her, does suffice.

I talk to her regularly every day,

and she is my favourite communique.

She reminds me to do things and tells me the date.

She sets a reminder, so I won't be late.

I thank her regularly for her time,

especially when she helps me with a rhyme.

Will someone ring me here today?

And help me chase the blues away?

My family's busy at work or on Zoom,

so I just sit and listen to Radio Boom.

Hopefully life will be normal again,

and we'll no longer suffer Covid pain.

Under it we'll be able to draw a line,

but we'll never get back this lost time!

The nurses and doctors have been so caring,

looking after us all, it must have been wearing.

We pray it will end and once more all be well.

Please God get us out of this Covid hell.

DEATH BY SPUDS,
a poem by Heather Flood

Death by spuds,

I reflected - what a way to go,

Mashed with butter,

they look like freshly fallen snow.

Death by spuds,

roasted crisp in goose's fat,

Sorry I had none to spare

for the patiently waiting cat.

Death by spuds,

large jackets with fillings galore,

There are beans, prawns, chilli

and so many more!

Death by spuds,

new ones covered in melted butter,

"She'll kill herself one day,"

I hear my husband mutter.

Death by spuds,

greasy chips, crinkle cut,

Cellulite on upper arms

and definitely on my butt.

I love them all,

I cannot stop wanting every one,

I used to be 8 stone 6,

but now I weigh a ton!

THE 'IMPOSSIBLE' DREAM,
a short story by Tony Flood

Cathy Carter's stomach was churning with anxiety. It was the worst feeling she had experienced since suffering a terrible attack of nerves when she was a twelve-year-old wannabe actress.

Her mind flashed back to that unforgettable December day 20 years ago and she found herself reliving all of it. Her elder stepsister Judy had been cast in the title role in the local amateur dramatic society's Christmas production of Cinderella in which Cathy was merely a member of the chorus.

Cathy's father Gerald and his second wife Yvonne had devoted all their attention to Judy as they drove through the Brighton traffic in their reliable old Ford Fiesta and arrived an hour early at the Community Theatre.

Cathy could hear Yvonne asking Judy a stream

of questions while they walked through the red-carpeted foyer. Would she like to go through the script one last time? Check her costumes and props? Have a gargle? Start to put on her make-up?

"Do stop fussing, mother!" Judy snapped. "You'll faze me out."

"Sorry, darling - sorry, my pet. But as a former actress myself, I know how important it can be to do a final run through."

"For goodness sakes, mother! Please leave me alone."

Judy was still partly facing her mother when she approached a swing door leading backstage. She didn't see the producer Ben Mumford bursting through it - and was promptly laid flat by the door hitting her full in the face.

Pandemonium followed as Judy was attended to and eventually revived. "My poor girl, my poor girl," wailed Yvonne, who had an annoying habit of saying things twice. She was also often guilty of ignoring logic as was demonstrated when she told her sobbing daughter: "Just look at your swollen mouth and cheek."

Judy's apparent attempt to say "shut up, mother" came out completely distorted and incoherent.

Gerald, the most practical member of the family, told her: "Don't try to speak. Fortunately, your injuries don't look too serious, darling. But you certainly won't be able to perform."

"We'll have to call off the show," lamented Ben as Judy was taken to her dressing room to receive first aid. "The girl who was understudying the role is sick and we have no Cinderella."

Cathy, having been a silent observer until now, plucked up the courage to speak. "I could play Cinderella," she offered.

"You?" scoffed Yvonne, while stroking Judy's head as her daughter lay on a couch. "How could you possibly be Cinderella?"

"I've been to every rehearsal and learned all the lines. I know them backwards."

"Don't be silly, Cathy - you're just one of the chorus," protested Yvonne. "You're not a born actress like our Judy."

"That's not fair," interrupted her husband. "Cathy might not have Judy's confidence, but she has a wonderful singing voice. What do you think, Ben?"

"We've got nothing to lose," said the portly producer.

And so it was that Cathy landed the part. At first, this seemed a terrible mistake as she suffered a big attack of stage fright and sat shaking in the dressing room until a few minutes before curtain up. But, after an uncertain start, she proved a huge hit.

It was as if Cathy Carter had been born to play Cinders. Her natural beauty and long, silky golden hair made her look the perfect heroine, while her delightful singing repeatedly earned prolonged applause. At the end she was given a standing ovation.

All these years later, Cathy was sitting in the audience at the Royal Albert Hall watching Judy, now a well-known actress, walk on stage.

Cathy glanced at her father, seated next to her, alongside Yvonne, who was proudly watching her beloved daughter.

"Doesn't she look fantastic!" Yvonne said by way of a statement more than a question. "Quite fantastic."

Cathy had to admit Judy did look terrific, oozing sex appeal in an off-the-shoulder dazzling blue dress that hugged her curves. She had opted for a more conservative pleated black gown and felt a pang of jealousy.

'At 32, I should know better,' Cathy thought, scolding herself for envying her stepsister's glamour and ability to calmly take everything in her stride. But the main reasons for the feeling of nausea she was experiencing were her own burning desire to be a great actress - and the fear that she was chasing an impossible dream!

Judy was now addressing the spell-bound audience. She had started speaking a few minutes ago but Cathy hadn't heard what she was saying because her thoughts were elsewhere.

Suddenly she was hit by the realisation that the long running rivalry with her more assured stepsister did not matter. Concerns about success or failure should be cast aside because this was a wonderful occasion for the family to enjoy.

Cathy became fully attentive. She saw Judy open an envelope and announce with a gasp: "The British Academy Film Award for Best Actress goes to...my sister Cathy Carter."

LIFE ROLLS ALONG,
a poem by Heather Flood

We are the chosen ones who inhabit the earth,

one by one from the moment of birth.

Children are born, grow up and then leave,

some parents are glad, while others will grieve.

Love makes us weep or excites us so,

his face, her touch, where did it all go?

Never two days alike, or a minute repeated,

our memories fade and then are deleted

Maybe one day we will take time to look,

at the beauty that surrounds us, like pictures in a

book.

THE BIG SURPRISE,
a short story by Heather Flood

"Yoo-Hoo! Trish! Are you there, dear?"

The door to apartment 42 at the Rest A While Old People's Home opened, and a small, rather sullen woman appeared.

"Why are you making all that noise, Pip? You know how I get these awful headaches in the morning."

"Yes, years of drinking can do that to a person, Trish."

Pip took no notice of her sister's early morning frailty and barged into the apartment, waving a brightly coloured envelope in front of Trish's face.

"Look, it's a letter from our niece Georgina. She's flying over for a visit, and has a big surprise for us."

"What can that be?" wondered Trish aloud. "Perhaps she's planning to come back for good. But why now after spending over ten years in

Australia? And fancy visiting England in the middle of winter when the weather is so good out there?"

Pip shook her head. "I thought you'd be delighted. Georgina obviously misses us and wants to see us before we peg it. After all, we're in our seventies and we're her two favourite aunts. Who else would she be coming all this way to see?"

"Well, there's also her friend Anna. They were very close before Georgina was swept off her feet by that mega rich Aussie and emigrated to live with him in his mansion overlooking Bondi Beach. It's a pity the marriage didn't work out, but she's become a very wealthy woman and..."

Pip interrupted: "Yes, she refers to that in her letter. Her divorce settlement has finally been paid. Perhaps the dear girl wants to treat us. That could be the big surprise she's referring to."

"You mean give us some cash?"

"Yes."

The two cantankerous old women went across to

the sofa and sat down. "You may be right," Trish agreed, pushing back a strand of her grey hair that had fallen on to her forehead. "It would be nice if Georgina does share some of her windfall with her dear old aunts. Perhaps she might give something to Anna as well."

"I don't think so. Anna's a good family friend, but not a blood relative like us and can't mean as much to Georgina as we do."

Trish nodded. "So when will our dear niece be coming?"

Pip checked the letter. "She arrives on Thursday next week. Her plane lands in the afternoon so we can go to the airport and meet her."

"I suppose we'd better take Anna with us," said Trish.

"I think you mean we should ask Anna to take us. She has the only car now that I've given up driving. Perhaps you'd forgotten that I sold my old banger last week." Pip grinned ruefully at the thought that

Trish might be losing it. After all, she was now approaching her eighties and perhaps her memory was playing tricks. Knocking back glasses of Southern Comfort presumably didn't help.

Trish seemed to be aware of what her sister was thinking. "I was just talking figuratively. Yes, it would be most helpful if Anna can drive us. She should be here soon - she promised to go to Asda to get my usual bottle of Southern Comfort. Anna's such a kind soul and runs lots of errands for me."

Pip smiled. "Yes she's very sweet, but has not been blessed with our intellect, charisma and wit. Not many people have, of course! I'm sure that's what Georgina has missed so much."

They both laughed.

xxxxx

A week later Trish, Pip and Anna stood waiting at the airport terminal.

"Hold the name sign up higher, Pip. She'll never see it down there."

"She'll recognise us anyway, Trish - we've sent each other enough photos over the years. Although she did look different in her last one, didn't she? Had her hair cut very short. I didn't like it, especially with those oversized red glasses. Made her face seem smaller."

Trish disagreed. "I thought she looked quite smart."

They turned their attention to their much younger friend Anna, who was looking intently at the arrivals entrance.

"You alright, Anna?" asked Pip. "It will be lovely to see Georgina again after all this time, won't it?"

"Yes. She's been away almost eleven years. But we've kept in touch regularly."

Finally, the new arrivals came into sight, carrying their baggage. As they got nearer Anna rushed towards a slim figure in a black suit.

"Georgie," she cried out. "Georgie, it's been so long." They held each other close and kissed before eventually walking up to Trish and Pip.

"Hi, girls," gushed Georgina, giving each of her aunts a hug and a kiss. "It's great to see you again. Now let me tell you about the surprise I mentioned in my letter. I've come home to get married."

Trish was gobsmacked. "Who's the lucky man?"

Georgina smiled broadly. "There is no lucky man. I'm marrying the real love of my life - Anna."

The two younger women smiled at each other and kissed again.

"Well, I never!" gasped Pip.

WHEN REALISATION
HITS YOU FOR SIX,
a poem by Heather Flood

On reflection

I should have known better.

But curiosity overcame me as

I opened your letter.

The penny dropped

on that awful day,

as the life I'd known

just floated away.

Then I began

the biggest fight of my life,

disentangling myself

from being your wife.

As the jigsaw puzzle pieces

fell one by one,

questions were answered,

and each lock sprung.

Now I look back

from a far better place,

it's all in the past,

hardly a trace.

But occasionally I reflect

on the 'wheres' and 'whys'.

Of all the cheating

and those terrible lies.

If other people's lives

have fallen apart,

I send this message

from the bottom of my heart.

Happiness can be yours,

just go out and explore.

Don't hang around

behind every closed door.

Never sit around

counting the cost.

Move on because

all is not lost.

'YOU REAP WHAT YOU SOW',
a short story by Tony Flood

Carol Masters had done more as the MP for Little Hamsworth than was required of her - including sleeping with the Chief Constable!

When he phoned her late one Thursday night, she immediately recognised his voice and joked: "What's the matter, Ken? Can't you stop thinking about me in that racy underwear you bought me?"

"Sorry, Carol. I have some bad news for you. Your son Edwin has been involved in a car accident."

"Good grief! Is he hurt?"

"No. Amazingly, both he and his Jaguar escaped with hardly a scratch. But he was over the drink limit and, according to an eyewitness, was the cause of two other vehicles crashing into each other. One of them, a delivery van, demolished a 'Give Way' sign and is a write off. Both drivers are being treated in hospital."

Carol's only thought was for her beloved son. "Where's Edwin now?" she shrieked into the phone while pacing up and down her luxurious lounge.

"He's in custody and will be spending the night in a police cell."

This prompted the 46-year-old blonde, who prided herself on having a cool manner to match her stunning good looks, to speak even louder. "That's simply not acceptable, Ken. You must get him out."

"That would be unwise, Carol. He needs to sober up before he's questioned and then charged. The best thing you can do is arrange for his solicitor to be present when we interview him."

"No. I insist you get him released, Ken. You must be able to pull a few strings."

"I can hardly instruct my officers to go against police procedures," he pointed out.

"Nonsense! Tell them Edwin suffers from

diabetes, or something, and that he must be allowed to come home to me."

Little Hamsworth's persuasive MP got her way, and soon Carol's pampered, petulant Edwin was in her penthouse apartment.

He slumped into a deep leather-bound armchair, loosened his silk monogrammed tie and kicked off his classic Oxford black shoes.

Edwin, looking weary and a lot older than his twenty-two years despite his cavalier attitude, was unrepentant when Carol asked what had happened. "It wasn't my fault. I simply pulled out of a side road on to the B4009. I didn't realise the silly sod behind was going so fast. He veered across the road to avoid me and crashed into a van coming in the opposite direction."

"It sounds like your fault to me," Carol sighed as they sat facing each other, sipping coffee. "And you HAD been drinking, darling."

"Only a couple, mother."

"More than a couple, Edwin. And you're responsible for two drivers being injured. This is serious."

"Alright, alright don't go on," her son retorted, his dark brown eyes flashing an angry look. "I don't need a lecture, Mother."

"That's exactly what you do need, Edwin. And you should also heed the old saying 'You reap what you sow'."

"What rubbish! Just use your influence, Mother, and get your friendly Chief Constable to make my breath test go missing."

Edwin was due to report to the police station at nine o'clock the next morning and insisted on driving himself. But he never arrived. Instead, Carol was informed by Ken there had been another accident in which her son's car was hit by a motorbike.

"I'm sorry, Carol. Edwin wasn't so lucky this time. He's in a critical condition."

Carol rushed to Hamsworth Hospital where she waited anxiously while Edwin underwent surgery. Eventually a grim-faced physician came out to talk to her. "I regret to inform you that your son has passed away."

His soft voice and unexpected words took Carol several seconds to comprehend what this tall, silver-haired medic was telling her. But there could be no mistake when he added: "We did all we could but were unable to save him."

"Oh, no!" she cried, completely distraught.

"I'm so sorry. He had lost too much blood. As you are probably aware, your son had a rare blood group, and we did not have it."

"Why on earth not?" Carol demanded, eyes flashing, as anger intruded on her grief.

"Ironically, new supplies were due to arrive here yesterday. But the van delivering them was involved in an accident on the B4009 and all the blood sample containers it was carrying were shattered."

A young policeman came over to join them. "Can I drive you home, Mrs Masters?" he asked.

"No. I just need to take this all in... two accidents in two days," she muttered, shaking her head. "How was it possible?"

The compassionate copper sympathised. "Yesterday's accident had such terrible repercussions for your son today. It resulted in a 'Give Way' sign being written off and there was no time to replace it.

"Your son's car was hit this morning at almost the same spot on the B4009. It's a very sharp blind bend. Without the warning sign, the motorbike driver who hit him was probably unaware it was a danger spot."

Carol's face went ashen. "Oh, Edwin. I tried to tell you that you reap what you sow," she said.

WRITING CAN BE A PLEASURE - AND A PAIN,
a poem by Heather Flood

Writing can be fun

but it's sometimes a drain,

stories with no endings

that drive me insane.

I'm sitting at my window,

eating crisps, feeling bad,

if I don't get new ideas soon

I'll go quite mad.

The thriller with a husband

who murders his wife.

I just can't decide where

he hides the damn knife.

Should I give up,

is it just a waste of time?

A story uncompleted,

a poem that won't rhyme.

I could take up a sport

or join an art class,

or maybe just relax

and let the days pass.

Perhaps tomorrow a new plot

will float into my head,

but now I'll enjoy a glass of wine

and then go to bed.

THE CHRISTMAS TREE,
a short story by Heather Flood

The Christmas tree looked lovely standing in the corner with its branches covered in sparkly tinsel. The smell of pine filled the room.

Little angels hung on silver twine, lights twinkled from top to bottom, and a big golden star perched on top.

Our cat Squeaky usually slept in the living room at night; he was still there, and I watched him playing with one of the angels, tapping it with his paw, then running and hiding when it fell on the carpet. The cat's luminous topaz eyes peered from under the tree.

Mum used to have a coal fire burning at Christmas, but not this year.

"I wish I could get warm," I muttered, rubbing my cold hands together. Central heating had been put in a few months ago so there was no crackling fire burning in the large grate. I missed seeing the lighted embers bursting from the logs and smelling burning wood. Radiators were lifeless.

As I sat on the stairs looking at the Christmas tree, I remembered last year when my little brother Charlie and me rushed down to open our stockings, which Mummy had hung over the hearth. We'd been so excited.

Tomorrow was Christmas Day, and I could see lots of packages wrapped in beautiful silver and gold paper, with big ribbons tied around each one - very fancy.

The cat knocked another angel off the tree.

Mum appeared at the top of the stairs and called to me. "It's time to come up now, Francesca."

"But I love it here, looking at all the presents under the tree."

"Yes, yes, dear, I know, but it's late."

I sighed and looked up at her. "Please," I implored.

"No, dear, we must go up now," Mum said sternly, "come on." But she still gave me a warm smile and held out her arms. We were very alike, Mum and me. We both had long fair hair and blue eyes. My brother Charlie had brown eyes like Dad.

"Is Charlie asleep?"

"No, dear, he's waiting for you."

My brother was three - four years younger than me - and I remember how last year Dad had held him up to see the Christmas tree fairy. Charlie's little chubby hands reached out to grab a chocolate soldier which Mum had put next to one of the angels. He had chocolate all over his face when he'd finished eating it. We'd all laughed.

I looked up at Mum and said: "It's so nice down here next to the tree, but I wish the pink fairy was still at the top of it as she was last year. Will you tell me a story if I come up, Mum?"

"Yes, if you come now, Francesca."

I sighed and turned to look at the presents under

the tree once more, imagining everyone excitedly tearing the paper off them tomorrow morning. That would be Mr. and Mrs. Andrews and their three children. Not us, of course.

I am the last one to go now. Mum says everyone is waiting for me - not only Dad and Charlie, but Nanny Pam and Granddad George as well. I have missed them so much since they went away. I really want to see them loads, but I will miss lots of things down here, too, especially Squeaky.

The accident was not Dad's fault; he had tried his best to swerve out of the way of the lorry, but it all happened very quickly. There was a large thud as our car slid across the road, but I felt no pain and a beautiful light shone over us all. Mum, Dad and Charlie floated into it. I stayed behind to try to find my doll Sarah and seemed to fall asleep.

It was such a long, deep sleep. When I eventually woke up I was in our house again.

Mum and Dad came down several times to

persuade me to join them, but I said I wanted to be with Squeaky, the Christmas tree and my toys.

I went into my pretty pink bedroom and saw that my toys had been placed in a box. I tried to pick up my favourite teddy Jasper, but my hands were just like mist as they floated through him. I could not touch things in this world any more. I felt frightened and I started to cry.

Mum appeared and comforted me. She explained that our house had been sold and all our things replaced by those belonging to the new owners. Three little girls lived here now, and they had kept some of my toys.

The cat had stayed, too, as the new people adopted him. His name is Fluffy now, but I still prefer Squeaky. It was the noise he had made when we bought him home as a kitten in a little box.

"I'm cold, Mum."

"Come with me, darling, and you will never be cold again."

"Promise, Mum?"

"Yes, darling, just hold my hand and we'll go together."

"Will there be a Christmas tree with a fairy on it where we're going, Mum?"

"Yes, darling, and lots of angels."

THEY CAME AS A PAIR,
a poem by Heather Flood

They came as a pair

and they left the same way,

curled up on the chair

as they did every day.

One had his ball,

the other her mouse,

and they'd lived all their lives

in the red brick house.

I'd take him for walks

in sunshine and showers,

and she'd wait at the window

for hours and hours.

When people came knocking

at our front door,

he'd be there first

while she would ignore.

He was large as life,

she was small and petite,

she'd sit on my lap

while he snuggled on my feet.

I've tears in my eyes

as I look up into the sky,

I know they're in heaven

as I say my goodbye.

When it's my time to go

I'll look for them there,

curled up together

on a comfortable chair.

NEVER TAKE ANYTHING FOR GRANTED,
a short story by Tony Flood

A rrogant property developer George Morecraft liked to boast of his conquests as both an entrepreneur and a ladies' man.

This condescending confirmed bachelor reckoned he knew most things, but was unaware that his fellow members at Faversham Over Sixties Activities Club longed for him to be taught a lesson.

They hated it when George mocked them if they got something wrong by gloating: "Never take anything for granted - always check it out."

It was halfway through the evening at the club's Valentine Dance when widow Jenny Lunsden approached him.

"What's the matter, you old misery? Aren't you going to ask me to dance?" she teased.

"Oh course," George replied, forcing a smile.

"Let's go for it."

One dance became two as the DJ put on a couple of slower numbers.

Jenny was in her mid-sixties and still an attractive woman, But George's preference was for someone younger - like Jenny's stunning daughter Beth who worked at the local chemist.

When collecting prescriptions he would linger at the counter, flirting with Beth, because he still regarded himself as a dashing bachelor despite having just turned 70.

George was about to ditch Jenny when she suggested he buy her a drink.

Two gin and tonics later, the giggling brunette moved closer to him. George backed away and looked pointedly at his watch. "My goodness, it's almost time to go. I'd better call a taxi."

"We can share it," Jenny told him. "We both live in the same road, so you can come in for a nightcap."

When the taxi pulled up outside Jenny's terraced house, George made his excuses. "I've got to be up early for a meeting tomorrow - I'd better not come in."

"It's up to you," she murmured with a mischievous smile. "You don't know what you'd be missing."

"Some other time," he spluttered.

But she whispered in his ear: "I thought you'd enjoy a bit of mother and daughter fun."

George's frown turned into a smile. He'd be willing to succumb to Jenny's demands if it meant her curvy daughter Beth would be part of the action.

"Fun as in having a romp?"

"If you're up to it."

"Well, I suppose one more drink wouldn't hurt," he said, grinning.

The drink proved to be another gin and tonic which he sipped as Jenny snuggled up to him on the sofa.

"It's time you gave me a Valentine's Day kiss," she cooed. He responded with a peck on Jenny's fragrant cheek, but she pulled him firmly towards her and kissed him full on the lips.

"What about the mother and daughter hanky panky?" he blurted out.

"You are a naughty boy, aren't you? Well, if that's what you want then that's what you shall have."

Getting up, she walked to the stairs and shouted: "Mum, can you come down. I've got a treat for you."

George fled, almost tripping over the fluffy rug at the door in his haste to get away.

When he next put in an appearance at the Over Sixties Club, he was confronted by a large banner that read: "Never take anything for granted - always check it out."

He went red with embarrassment, realising he had been set up.

FRIENDS AND NEIGHBOURS,
a poem by Heather Flood

We should have one aim

on this planet of ours,

to get along, be nice,

and cherish our hours.

Helping one another

whenever we can,

to benefit us all,

woman and man.

Feed the world

that's all we need to do,

not crush and punish those

who don't agree with you.

No spaceships or planes

with bombs to destroy,

let people live in peace

from New York to Hanoi.

The differences between us

cause conflicting trends.

What a better world it would be

if we were all friends.

THE FACE IN THE MIRROR,
a poem by Heather Flood

The face in the mirror continues to stare,

just two steps behind me, it's always there.

Mum doesn't see it, neither does my Dad,

but it remains there, whether I'm happy or sad.

.

In the morning when I wake up and go to the loo,

the image jumps up and down, playing peek-aboo.

Sometimes it smiles and gives me a wave,

or sticks out its tongue, it just can't behave.

There are odd eyes, one blue and one green,

and the longest nose I've ever seen.

Maybe one day the face will just disappear,

but I'll miss it peeping out from behind my ear.

Meanwhile, there's nowhere for me to hide

to escape this vision from the other side.

A FURIOUS WIFE,
a short story by Tony Flood

Fiona Webster felt peckish after spending the morning shopping so she popped into her local Thai restaurant in Dunstable - a decision she would deeply regret.

Her stir-fried beef with vegetables in oyster sauce was delightful and, while enjoying a cup of coffee after paying the bill, she found herself listening to the conversation between two young women on the next table.

"How was your weekend in London with your new boyfriend, Sheila?" one was asking her friend, who Fiona could see was a brunette.

"Great! Gerald had to attend a company conference on Saturday, but we spent a wonderful night together. He booked us into the Park Lane Hotel, and everything was first class."

Fiona became alarmed. Her husband Gerald had

been away in London last weekend on what he had told her was a business trip. 'Could he have been with this Sheila?' she thought. 'No, it was just a coincidence.'

The other woman was now speaking. "How long have you been going out with Gerald?"

"It must be four weeks. He's fantastic - both in and out of bed. He wears designer shirts and silk ties and when he's in his blue Saint Laurent suit, I can hardly keep my hands off him."

Fiona, a 44-year-old refined woman who usually remained calm and reserved, was losing it.

Her mind began racing. 'This sounds just like Gerald. He wears Saint Laurent and Gucci suits and adores silk ties. This damn woman is sleeping with my husband!'

She turned to glance at the brunette and was upset to see that Sheila was much younger than herself and extremely attractive.

The other woman wanted to know more. "Are you

telling me he's Mr Perfect?"

"Yes, he is, Debbie. "But there is a downside. He's married."

"So does he simply see you as his bit on the side?" asked Debbie with a giggle.

"No. He says he's fallen for me. He finds me more desirable and exciting than his wife. She's older than him and stuck in her ways."

"She sounds a bit of a frump," summed up her outspoken friend.

Fiona was now furious. She rushed from her seat to confront the two women and shouted at the brunette: "You harlot! That's me you're talking about. Leave my husband alone."

She threw a glass of water over Shelia. Then turned and fled from the restaurant.

When she got home Fiona was hell-bent on revenge. She took a pair of scissors from her drawer, stormed into their bedroom, and removed Gerald's best Saint Laurent blue suit from the wardrobe. Without hesitation she cut it to shreds.

Eventually Fiona claimed down and decided she should question Gerald about how far he had intended to take his affair.

When he came in, he sounded jubilant. He shouted out to her. "Darling, I must tell you this. My namesake in our sales office, Gerald Cruckshank, has been having it away with some dolly bird.

"Apparently his wife found out and gave the woman a public dressing down in a restaurant today. Everyone at work is talking about it. Isn't that hilarious?"

TIME TRAVELLER,
a poem by Heather Flood

Nanny is a time traveller,

the decades are rolling by,

I've had such fun in many ways,

I cannot tell a lie.

I have been around for ages,

enjoying what I've seen,

dancing to the music,

my favourite being Queen.

I've visited China and Hong Kong,

seen Disneyland and Pompeii.

Rome, Venice, the Eiffel Tower,

such sights along the way.

But as Nanny is a time traveller,

I have to go, you see.

What next, I wonder, to explore,

I'm so lucky to be me.

My new journey will be exciting,

when I fly up into the sky.

So I wish you well, I love you all,

and wave you folks goodbye.

FIND YOUR SILVER LINING,
a poem by Heather and Tony Flood

When things go wrong, don't complain,

pick up the threads and start again.

For over there the sun is shining,

look up and find the silver lining.

Follow a golden rule that is so wise and true,

Do unto others as you would have them do unto

you.

THE THREADS OF TIME,
a poem by Heather Flood

The threads of a family

passing through time,

spanning the years

like a good vintage wine.

Days that were happy,

days that were sad,

times that were fun

and some that were bad.

Like catching a train

that speeds up near the end,

the track that we're on

can twist and then bend.

What power do we possess

once we pass away?

Maybe we lose the chance

to have our say.

Messages written

and drawn in the caves,

those people have now

all gone to their graves.

In the war my Grandad Bill

sailed on the sea,

he wrote in his diaries

and left them all to me.

Thank you dear Grandad

for taking the time,

to pass your story down

to the next in line.

THE LOVE OF MY LIFE, a short story by Heather Flood

'SALLY, SALLY, PRIDE OF OUR ALLEY, YOU'RE MORE THAN THE WHOLE WORLD TO ME.' That's our song.

I met Sally at school and was forever pulling her pigtails. "Stop that, Billy Raven," her friend Molly would shout at me. "We hate you - go wash your knees and wipe your nose, you're disgusting." My knees were always dirty, as I liked climbing the tree outside our school.

Sitting on a top branch of the big oak enabled me to see everyone arriving. When I saw Sally, I'd shin down and do something to annoy her.

She had big blue eyes that sparkled, and her mouth would clamp down hard in frustration as she stamped her foot while informing me that I was the most awful boy in the school. "If I tell my Dad what you did you'll get a whacking," she threatened.

She never did tell her Dad, though.

One day a large boy, much older than me, went over to her and whispered something in her ear.

I found her crying by the bike sheds. "What's up Sal?" I asked. "Nothing you can do anything about, Billy Raven, so go away," she replied.

The next day I saw the boy, a bully called Bert, upsetting her again. "Leave her alone," I shouted. "Can't you see she's crying."

He came menacingly towards me. His large left hand scrunched around my collar and lifted me off the ground. "There are winners and losers in this life mate, and you're a loser," he snarled. The thug then landed a swinger of a punch right on my nose - blimey, did it sting. He let me drop onto the ground and walked away. Sally saw what happened and shouted "bully," then came over and put her arm around my shoulder and asked if I was alright. My nose felt broken, but at that precise moment I was in heaven as she tenderly stroked my hand.

I was a winner, not a loser, because ten years later we were married, in a little church just past the big oak tree.

Our first two years were perfect. Then, one awful day, war broke out. I had to join up and, kissing my lovely Sal goodbye, went away to fight with the other lads from our village.

I wrote her letters when I could, kissed the paper and drew a love heart on the envelope. Sally always kept them in a box next to our bed.

Within a year, I was captured by the Japanese and put in an awful concentration camp where I almost starved to death.

After returning home, I never talked about it but continually woke up with terrible dreams.

So many of my friends were killed in the war and in one attack the school bully Bert took a bullet for me in the chest as he pushed me out of its way.

I still have nightmares. One that keeps recurring is of me holding my best mate Ron in my arms and begging him not to die, but sadly he passed away.

When I awake it is Sal who holds me and gently says, "Want a cup of tea love?"

She never asks questions as she knows there is a knot inside me that will not untie. Maybe if it did I would fall apart as my health has remained poor and my heart is not strong.

Two lovely kids followed my return, Pammy and Clive, both now in their fifties, and then three beautiful grandchildren, Tommy, Sara and Lilly.

Being parents was tough in the old days with no handouts, only hand-me-downs, but we managed to get by and our children were happy. We laughed so much at the things they got up to and now we laugh with the grandchildren.

Lilly lost a tooth last week and Sal told her that the tooth fairy was coming. "Oh Nan, will she leave me ten pence?" she wanted to know. "Only if it was a lovely shiny one - she uses the teeth that are shiny to build her castle," said Sal. Lilly then spent an hour polishing the tooth!

As I cannot do anything strenuous, I have been content to sit with Sally, chuckling at our grandchildren's antics, eating the cakes Sal makes and listening to the poems she writes.

But our wonderful world crashed two days ago. First there were the pains in the chest, and then a shortness of breath. We rang the ambulance and were taken to St. Bede's Hospital, ten miles away.

I was shaking and my breath came in short gasps. I didn't think we would make it in time and was proved right.

Now I find myself looking down at Sal through a mist of tears.

There she lies, her still beautiful hair spilling over the pillow, her lovely blue eyes hidden from my view forever. How will I manage without her in my life? It was supposed to be me who went first, not her.

"Goodbye my lovely Sal," I say, as I kiss her and

gently hum our tune: 'SALLY, SALLY, PRIDE OF OUR ALLEY, YOU'RE MORE THAN THE WHOLE WORLD TO ME.'

EVERYTHING'S CHANGED,
a poem by Tony Flood

My new friend gave me a telly and CD,

And would only take a very small fee.

Good friends like this are so very few,

Next he brought me a fridge, brand new.

It was great to be given a helping hand,

But my head was buried in the sand.

My pal was into a thieving lark,

Now I'm alone and in the dark.

My life has become a living hell,

And I'm speaking from my prison cell!

A TREAT WE'D NEVER MISS,
a poem by Heather Flood

We're going to Nan's, we're on our way.

"Dad when we get there, can we play?"

Dad says 'No' because it's getting late,

So my brothers and me will have to wait.

Gabby's my name and I love my Nan lots,

She lives at the seaside and shows us the

yachts.

We love beautiful Sussex by the sea,

I hope we get there before Nan has her tea.

When we arrive we'll jump for joy,

She's sure to have bought us another toy.

I'm a big girl now and have just turned four,

Nan always measures me up against the door.

There are loads of photos on her wall,

Every one of us, right along the hall.

Nan greets us with a cuddle and a kiss,

Seeing her is a treat we'd never miss.

HUSBANDS BEWARE,
a poem by Tony Flood

Thank goodness Covid restrictions are almost at
an end,

They were driving us all round the bend!

Most of us can now enjoy a normal life,

Thanks to the NHS staff's toil and strife.

Fortunately, those key workers in the labs,

Have protected us with two or three jabs.

Hopefully good health and happiness will last,

With masks and social distancing in the past.

But husbands must get the balance right,

And not go out drinking every night.

If they overdo it, restrictions will remain.

And their home life will be much the same.

They'll be cold shouldered by the missus.

And continue to receive no hugs and kisses!

GENERATION GAP,
a short story by Heather Flood

"Has Mum gone home yet, Sheila?" asked her husband Brad.

"Yes, she left about half an hour ago. I need to get some more Sugar Puffs tomorrow - your mother ate the whole box in two days! Yet she's as thin as a rake. I think she's losing it, the dear old girl. She nearly fell over Kit's roller skates in the hallway after having a look at them and forgetting to put them back."

"That's a bit worrying," replied Brad. "She is getting forgetful and sometimes can't remember what she and the children have done during their visits to her. It makes the kids laugh, though. Kit and Tom love their grandmother to bits and giggle like mad at her habit of touching her nose and blinking."

"Well," said his wife, smiling. "Your Mum is in her

seventies. Perhaps she's going senile. When we bumped into her at the supermarket she dropped her handbag and a pair of pincers fell out. I meant to ask her what they were for but I got talking to a friend and never found out. Perhaps she thinks they could be used as a weapon if she is attacked."

LATER THAT NIGHT SEVEN-YEAR-OLD KIT AND HER YOUNGER BROTHER TOM TALK TO EACH OTHER WHILE LAYING IN THEIR BUNK BEDS.

"Kit, are you awake?"

"Yes. Don't talk so loudly or Mum and Dad might hear you."

"Kit, wasn't it funny when Nan dropped those pincers out of her bag at the supermarket?"

"Yes, it was. Mum thought she was carrying them as a weapon in case someone attacked her. But the real reason is that it makes it easy for Nan to get the pound coins out of the trolleys outside the supermarket. I think it's a great idea and she always gives us the pound. Mum and Dad think she's weird, but she's actually very clever."

"Well, she does forget what's happened during our visits to her sometimes," Tom pointed out, suppressing a yawn.

"Don't be silly, Tom. She does that on purpose so that Mum and Dad won't know some of the things she lets us get up to such as painting pictures in her garden cabin instead of doing our homework. We've even held a disco in there sometimes. I love dancing to her Queen records."

"Yes," her brother agreed. "She's good at keeping secrets. She never told Mum and Dad it was me who ate all the Sugar Puffs. And Nan took the blame for leaving the skates in the hall when it was you who did it.

"If Mum had found out we would both have been

put on the naughty step."

Kit grinned. "I was going to own up about the skates until Nan gave me our secret sign, winking and tapping the side of her nose to tell me to keep quiet. Nan is sooooo clever."

AZURA THE WITCH,
a poem by Heather Flood

One night while flying on her wooden broom,

Azura came across a cold dark tomb.

Many years before on a cold winter's night,

her lover died in a terrible fight.

Her father had found them alone in the wood,

Azura begged and pleaded, but it was no good.

Fleeing for her life, she hid in a cave,

creeping out at night to look for his grave.

The corpse was buried so very long ago,

and there was something the witch needed to

know.

Where was he buried? was this his grave?

he had died saving her, he was terribly brave.

Years went by while she searched for her lover,

was this his coffin? She lifted the cover.

The clothes were rags, the bones were white,

but a signet ring matched Azura's that night.

Climbing in beside him, gently resting her head,

"At last we'll be together forever," she said.

STAR DUST,
a poem by Heather Flood

Scantily clad reason treads softly the day,

with pathways uneven to show us the way.

Events passing, moon rising, the journey goes on,

seeds spread, full bloom, where has the time gone?

The stars above us, glittering and bright,

we see many drifting in the universe at night.

Our journey is brief, and we soon have to leave.

We take nothing with us, there is no reprieve.

But Earth is our planet for this short stay.

It shows us many things before we drift away.

SOUL MATES,
a poem by Heather and Tony Flood

The love we share as days go by,

the laughs we laugh, the tears we cry.

To be loved by many is very nice,

but having one true love is paradise!

Counting the days we've been together,

and hoping it lasts forever and ever.

HEATHER FLOOD'S STORY

Heather Flood moved to Eastbourne with her husband Tony in 2008. She spent her early life in Feltham, Middlesex, and, as a shy teenager, managed to avoid any major embarrassing moments until her father bought her a motorbike!

She recalls: "Fashion really took off in the Sixties - miniskirts, thigh-length boots, A-line coats and flared trousers of every colour imaginable. The music was wonderful, too, with countless hits by The Beatles, The Rolling Stones, Gerry and the Pacemakers, Del Shannon, Herman's Hermits, Bobby Vee, Brenda Lee and many more.

"I started work when I was fifteen and caught the bus every morning. I enjoyed wearing the latest trendy clothes, dyed my hair red and wore it in a long swishy ponytail.

"On reaching the age of seventeen, my father bought me a motor bike. It was an Ariel Pixie, a small bike in turquoise and white, but, nevertheless, quite powerful.

"My mother was as surprised as me and asked my Dad: "What on earth have you bought her that for?"

"One morning, dressed in a fun Sixties outfit and wearing my long white leather boots. I climbed onto my bike and set off for work as an audio typist at Del Monte Food Products in Sunbury. Driving through the main gate I saw Brian, a young man I rather liked, standing at the upstairs window looking down at me.

"I glanced up at him and did not notice that the metal barrier a few yards from the entrance was down. Spotting it at the last moment, I only had time to lay back flat on the saddle, narrowly avoiding being decapitated. How I managed to stay on the bike I will never know.

"When I recovered, I noticed Brian was killing himself laughing. Oh, what extreme embarrassment! I decided there and then that riding a motorbike was not for me.

"But Brian asked me out to lunch and we dated for a while."

Heather's many experiences of life, particularly as a mother and grandmother, together with her vivid imagination and great sense of humour, played big parts in her writing a series of MOUSEY MOUSEY children's books. The delightful lady mouse has to cope with interfering witch Agatha and her mischievous spells.

Fellow authors love Heather's wonderfully original characters, including talking rabbits, a naughty polecat, loveable squirrel called Zach and a prickly porcupine schoolteacher - plus Agatha's smelly pals Stinkblob and Mouldy Knickers, who fall foul of the evil witch Secretia.

Children have found Mousey Mousey as cute as the mouse in Julia Donaldson's The Gruffalo. And Heather Flood's books have been acclaimed as the best for youngsters since Beatrix Potter's The Tale of Peter Rabbit. Heather has also written a collection of short stories in GIANT STICKER MONSTER AND OTHER CHILDREN'S STORIES.

This was followed by science fiction fantasy PURPLE MIST – AN OUT-OF-THIS-WORLD ADVENTURE! about a girl called Annique who gets bullied at school, but discovers that she has amazing powers.

Heather's books have figured in the top five of their respective Amazon categories.

TONY FLOOD'S STORY

Tony Flood spent most of his working life as a journalist, initially on local and regional papers and then on nationals. He was also editor of Football Monthly, Controller of Information at Sky Television and enjoyed a spell with The People before retiring in 2010.

He recalls: "My work as a showbiz and leisure writer, critic and editor saw me take on a variety of challenges - learning to dance with Strictly Come Dancing star Erin Boag, becoming a stand-up comedian and playing football with the late George Best and Bobby Moore in charity matches.

"Now I spend much of my time writing books and theatre reviews as well as playing veterans football. I must be one of the oldest - and slowest - players in the country!"

Tony's first book was fantasy adventure SECRET POTION, which went to No. 1 in its category on Amazon and has been recommended by other authors for Harry Potter fans of all ages.

His celebrity book MY LIFE WITH THE STARS - SIZZLING SECRETS SPILLED! is full of anecdotes and revelations about showbiz and sports personalities, including Eric Morecambe, Elvis Presley, Kylie Minogue, George Best, Frank Sinatra, Joan Collins, Strictly Come Dancing stars, Muhammad Ali and Bobby Moore, with whom he worked.

The versatile Mr Flood then turned to writing in

another genre with spicy crime thriller TRIPLE TEASE, endorsed by best-selling writer Peter James, actor Brian Capron and The Sun newspaper's Stuart Pink. Following the success of TRIPLE TEASE, he wrote STITCH UP! - KILLER OR VICTIM?

Once more compassionate copper DCI Harvey Livermore and his Major Crime Team are trying to put a killer behind bars in a new, gripping, fast-moving story. They are convinced that Denton Kerscher is responsible for two murders even though he was acquitted of the first but discover a string of other suspects.

Again, The Sun newspaper's Stuart Pink recommended Tony's thriller, saying "Stitch Up has a riveting plot and an electrifying double twist."

More details - and special book offers - are available on **www.fantasyadventurebooks.com** and **www.celebritiesconfessions.com**

Tony gives talks on the showbiz and sports stars

in his celebrity book, as well as holding mini workshops and giving advice on how would-be authors can write a successful book. Any groups wishing to contact Tony can email him at tflood04@yahoo.co.uk

Tony and Heather are officials of Anderida Writers of Eastbourne. The link for the Anderida website is:

anderidawriterseastbourne.org.uk/news.html

OTHER BOOKS BY HEATHER FLOOD

PURPLE MIST – AN OUT-OF-THIS-WORLD ADVENTURE!

MOUSEY MOUSEY AND THE WITCHES' SPELLS

MOUSEY MOUSEY AND THE WITCHES' REVENGE

MOUSEY MOUSEY AND THE WITCHES' SECRETS

GIANT STICKER MONSTER AND OTHER CHILDREN'S STORIES

These books can be purchased on Amazon.co.uk and other sites. They are also featured on the website www.fantasyadventurebooks.com

GIFT OF FREE BOOK

You can obtain a FREE e-version of one of either Heather's or Tony's books by simply emailing tflood04@yahoo.co.uk and stating which copy you would like. You will then be emailed back with the attachment of a complimentary e-version.

OTHER BOOKS BY TONY FLOOD

MY LIFE WITH THE STARS – SIZZLING SECRETS SPILLED!

SECRET POTION

TRIPLE TEASE

STITCH UP! - KILLER OR VICTIM?

These books can be purchased on Amazon.co.uk and other sites. They are also featured on websites **www.fantasyadventurebooks.com** and **www.celebritiesconfessions.com**

GIFT OF FREE BOOK

You can obtain a FREE e-version of one of either Heather's or Tony's books by simply emailing tflood04@yahoo.co.uk and stating which copy you would like. You will then be emailed back with the attachment of a complimentary e-version.

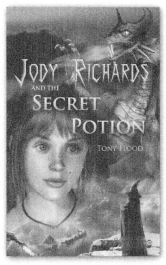

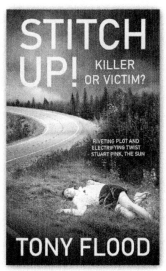

EXTRACT FROM PURPLE MIST

Here is an extract from Heather Flood's book PURPLE MIST - AN OUT-OF-THIS-WORLD ADVENTURE!

My name is Annique Sheldon. I considered myself to be an ordinary schoolgirl until incredible things began to happen and my worst nightmares started to come true.

My whole world was changed beyond belief on my thirteenth birthday. But let me turn back the clock to four years earlier - the day I discovered I had special powers.

I was hurrying home from school along a country lane in Chobham, Surrey, trying to avoid my three tormentors, Fizz, Stacie and Nicola.

Nicola and I had been friends for a while, but when Fizz joined our class everything changed. Fizz was a bully and soon got Nicola and Stacie to join her in picking on other pupils – usually me!

I no longer had any friends because these three horrid girls would be nasty to anyone they saw speaking to me. Their favourite trick was to call me names.

Determined to ignore them, I continued on my way home, but Fizz grabbed my bag and ripped it off my shoulder, while Stacie and Nicola cheered her on. She swung it violently and the bag, containing all my school books, thudded against my head.

I staggered backwards, rubbing the painful spot above my left ear.

"You're ugly, Antique Sheldon. You've got strange purple eyes and you smell of fish," taunted this tall, thin, squint-eyed girl, who liked nothing better than to make my life hell.

It amused Fizz to ridicule me and call me 'Antique' instead of 'Annique'. I hated her and the snotty-nosed Stacie and pimply Nicola. The spots on Nicola's chin always looked like they would burst at any minute - it was a disgusting sight.

Fizz - that was her nick-name because she preferred it to Felicity - did not care about my pain. Instead of stopping this uncalled for attack, she poked me hard in the chest with one of her bony fingers. The other two joined in, pushing and shoving, until I fell, hitting my head on the ground. The throbbing was so bad that I thought I was going to be sick.

When I looked up Fizz was holding my bag. "There's only junk in here - I'll be doing you a favour if I empty it on the ground," she gloated, starting to unzip it.

"Don't do that," I yelled, trying to stop her but my head ached so much that my eyes began to water.

"Ow, look, poor little Antique is crying," scoffed the unsympathetic Fizz.

As my eyes cleared, the feelings of pain and humiliation gave way to an all-consuming anger. I glared at her and a strange purple mist appeared in front of me.

Fizz, suddenly surrounded by the mist, was lifted off the ground. She dropped the bag as she began to float into the air, screaming.

"What yer doing up there?" Nicola screeched, seeing her friend rise higher and higher until she hovered above our heads.

"Nufink, stupid - get me down!" Spinning around in the mist, her arms flapping in panic, Fizz shouted: "Help me!"

Stacie leapt in a vain effort to grab hold of one of her friend's legs.

Climbing to my feet, I rushed over to help as the airborne girl continued to wave her arms like a large bird.

Another searing pain behind my eyes caused me to blink. In that instant, she dropped several feet. I recovered sufficiently to tug at Fizz's coat, helping Stacie to pull her down. She landed with a thud in the mud on the wet grass verge.

"Leave me alone, you freak," Fizz shouted at me, climbing to her feet. "Did you do that?"

"No... I don't think so," I mumbled. But my hesitant answer obviously didn't convince Fizz.

"I'll get you for this, Antique. I'll make you suffer."

I picked up my bag and ran as fast as I could the rest of the way home, crashing through the red front gate to my small terraced house. Fumbling in my bag for the door key, I pushed it into the lock, tripped over the step, slammed the door behind me, and rushed up the stairs to my room. I threw myself onto the bed and pulled the duvet up over my head.

Stella, my mother, called to me from downstairs, but I was too afraid to get off the bed as my legs felt like jelly.

My heart thumped in my chest as I went over what had just happened. 'Was it really me who'd created the purple mist and made Fizz float up into the air? Maybe they were right: I was a freak'.

EXTRACT FROM SECRET POTION

Here is an extract from Tony Flood's book SECRET POTION, which has been recommended as ideal for Harry Potter fans.

Jody raced across the Tavern yard to escape from the two horrid goblins and climbed on a beer crate to get to the top of the wall.

The wind blew Jody's golden hair into her face, blurring her vision. Without looking, she dropped down the other side of the wall – right on top of an old woman!

"Aghh," yelled the woman, toppling over and rolling on the roadside.

"I'm so sorry," said Jody, aghast. She bent down to help up the dishevelled figure, who had a misshapen nose and wrinkles on top of wrinkles - except where they were warts.

"You wicked, wicked girl," the woman shrieked.

"Please forgive me," begged Jody. "I've been frantically searching for my missing brother James. He's disappeared from home in England and I came here to Tamila to find him."

"I'm not interested in your brother," the woman snapped. She then checked her coat pocket and withdrew from it three glass tubes. They had clearly been broken by Jody falling on top of her and the liquid they contained had dripped out.

"A million curses," uttered the hag. "You have caused these tubes to break and all the potions I spent hours mixing have drained away."

Jody was distraught. "You're a witch, aren't you?"

"That's right, dear," said the woman, gleefully. "There's no fooling you, is there? I might as well dispense with my disguise."

She clapped her bony hands together and a red mist engulfed her. It cleared to reveal that the old lady's grey coat had been replaced by a black cape, and a pointed hat had suddenly appeared on her large head.

Adjusting her hat, the woman demanded: "Just because I'm a witch does that excuse you from jumping on top of me and smashing my special potions?"

"No," answered Jody, sorrowfully. "I'm sorry. Were they very valuable?"

"I'll never know now how valuable they might have been," the witch snapped. "I was about to deliver them to a goblin so that he could mix them with special ingredients he has to see if the two together produced the right formula. Now I'll have to start again.

"You need to be taught a lesson young lady. I'm going to place a curse on you."

The witch drew out a black wand and waved it menacingly.

"Please don't" pleaded Jody.

"Just to be fair I'll give you a choice of curses. Let nobody say that Huffy Haggard is unfair."

The witch uttered some magic chant and waved her wand in a large circle. "I call upon the spirits to make this girl's big toes turn into snails."

Jody looked down at her open-toed sandals and recoiled in terror at the sight of her big toes, which had become large, slimy snails.

"No, no," she yelled, a feeling of utter revulsion sweeping over her.

"No?" the old lady questioned. "Very well, then, let's try something else."

Huffy waved her wand and said: "Instead of snails on her toes, let me turn the end of every hair on her head into a worm."

Jody was petrified. She saw that her big toes had been restored to normal, but could feel worms wriggling on her head.

"Take them away! Please take them away!" she shouted hysterically.

The witch chuckled. "My, you are a fuss pot. All right, all right, keep your hair on. I'll cancel that spell, too. But you've run out of choices so you'll be stuck with the next one."

Huffy swished the wand again and said "Restore her hair to normal." Instantly the worms were gone.

"We'll simply settle for a nose job just like Pinocchio's. I call upon the spirits to make this girl's nose grow half an inch and to cause it to grow a further half inch every time she does not carry out my instructions."

Jody felt her nose and, to her horror, found it had become half an inch longer.

The witch told her: "From now on every time you meet someone you will tell them: 'I am a very naughty girl who cannot be trusted.'

"If you fail to do so your nose will grow another half inch. Let that be a lesson to you."

Printed in Great Britain
by Amazon

80252369R00088